BOBBIN'S LAND

By Carol Cornelius

**Illustrated by
Franz Altschuler**

THE
CHILD'S
WORLD

ELGIN, ILLINOIS 60120

Library of Congress Cataloging in Publication Data

Cornelius, Carol, 1942-
    Bobbin's land

    (A Concept book)
    SUMMARY: Follows the life of a robin family from their
arrival to their summer home in early spring to their
southern migration in late fall.
    1. Robins—Legends and stories.
    [1. Robins—Fiction. 2. Birds—fiction] I. Altschuler,
Franz. II. Title
PZ10.3.C8157Bo   [E]   78-2399
1SBN 0-913778-99-0

Distributed by Childrens Press, 1224 West Van Buren Street, Chicago,
Illinois 60607.

© 1978 The Child's World, Inc.

BOBBIN'S LAND

2091060

Spring was moving up from the South. With spring, came hundreds of birds. A young cock robin, named Bobbin, was one of the birds moving north with spring. He followed the great Mississippi River.

Bobbin was flying high above the trees when he spotted just what he was looking for. Down below, he saw an orchard, a field, and a creek with willow trees.

Bobbin made a smooth landing in the field. He was not the only bird there. A red-tailed hawk sailed back and forth overhead, looking for meadow mice. A blackbird pecked in the plowed field. Two mourning doves perched on a fence wire.

Bobbin sang to announce his arrival and to see if the property belonged to any other robin. No other robin came to drive him away. Bobbin was the only robin there.

So he flew up onto a fencepost and sang this song:

"My land! My land!
Fly away, fly away!
I will fight you if you stay!"

The days grew warmer, and with the warmer
weather came more robins. Bobbin never let
any other bird with a red breast stay on his land.
When another robin landed, Bobbin would fly up
to hit him. He'd puff out his bright red breast and
screech:

"My land! Fly away!
I will fight you if you stay!"

The new robin usually left immediately.

But one day a robin didn't fly away. She was a hen. Her name was Cherrie. Cherrie didn't want to fight. She acted as if she were a baby robin, begging for a worm. Bobbin could not help finding a worm for her.

Cherrie and Bobbin became mates. He took her on a flying tour of his land. He showed her the orchard, the field, and the creek with willow trees.

Cherrie thought the orchard was a fine place to
build a nest. She picked out a low, forked branch
in an apple tree.

Cherrie knew how to build a strong nest. First
she brought a load of dead grass and dropped it
on the forked branch. Then she sat down and
pressed the mud into the dead grass.

For six days, Cherrie worked to build the nest.
She carried loads and loads of grass and mud.
She pressed and pressed until the nest was perfect.

Bobbin was not much help in building the nest.
He sang happily while Cherrie worked.

When the nest was ready, Cherrie laid one small, blue-green egg every day for five days. Bobbin was very happy. Here is the song he sang:

"Bobbin cock robin am I,
owner of all that you see—
an orchard, a nest,
five eggs, and the best
wife that ever could be!
Cherrie! Cherrie! Cherrie!"

For twelve days, Bobbin sang wonderful songs about his land, his nest, his eggs, and his wife.

Cherrie was happy but quiet. She sat on the eggs to keep them warm. She turned them with her feet and bill, so the eggs stayed warm all over.

On the thirteenth day, five chicks without feathers pecked their way out of the blue-green eggs.

Now Bobbin didn't have time to sing. Every time he looked at his five chicks, he saw five wide-open, empty mouths. The five baby robins could eat hundreds of worms a day! Bobbin and Cherrie had to work hard to find that many worms.

At night, Cherrie slept sitting on the nest. She covered the babies and kept them warm.

Bobbin slept perched on a branch near the nest.

The five baby robins grew fatter and fluffier every day. They were restless in the small nest.

Once Bobbin came home with a load of green tomato worms. He found all the babies out of the nest and perched on a branch. The little robins had their wing feathers now. They were always stretching to try out their wings.

One day, all five baby robins jumped into the
air together, fluttering awkwardly to the ground.
They never returned to the nest, not even at night.

Bobbin and Cherrie had to find the chicks to
feed them. The young robins got lost in the
weeds and bushes. They peeped loudly until
Bobbin or Cherrie found them and stuffed them
with worms.

A fox lived in the brushy fence row across the field. One day, he heard a baby robin chirping in the grass. He ran to gobble it up!

Cherrie screeched and dove at the fox, hitting him with her wings. Bobbin zoomed down and pecked the fox on the head. All the other birds in the orchard screeched loudly.

The fox slunk off into the brush, still hungry.

25

After about a week, the five young robins had
learned to fly very well. They were picking their
own cherries from the orchard trees. They could
even pull their own worms out of the ground.

Bobbin had time to sing again. He sang
wonderful songs, because the orchard in the
summertime was a wonderful place to be.

But he didn't have long to sing. He and Cherrie
had a second family to raise that summer. Five
more babies hatched, grew up, and flew away.

Then it was autumn. Days were growing shorter. Bobbin's and Cherrie's new red breast feathers came in tinged with grey. These were their traveling feathers. Soon they would be flying South.

One day, Cherrie could wait no longer. She was full of ripe berries and furry caterpillars. She could fly a long way without stopping to eat. She left Bobbin singing in the warm, bug-buzzing orchard.

This was the song she heard as she flew away.

"This is Bobbin's land,
and I'll be here
come next year.
I'll be here
in this orchard,
by this field,
near this creek with willow trees,
on my land,
beautiful Bobbin land!"

Then he too flew away.